Japanese Fairy Tales

VOLUME 4

Stories by Keisuke Nishimoto
Illustrations by Yoko Imoto

HEIAN

© 1997 Text by Keisuke Nishimoto / Illustrations by Yoko Imoto
Originally published in Japan by Kodansha Ltd.
© 2000 English Edition by Heian International, Inc. USA

HEIAN INTERNATIONAL, INC.
1815 West 205th Street, Suite #301
Torrance, CA 90501

First American Edition 2000
10 9 8 7 6 5 4 3 2 1

Translated by Dianne Ooka
Edited by Charisse Vega

ISBN: 0-89346-930-0

Web site:www.heian.com
E-mail: heianemail@heian.com

Printed in Hong Kong

Table of Contents

VOLUME 4

The Monkey and the Crab.   4

The Gold Coin Drying Field.   14

Gonbei the Duck Hunter.   16

The Cat and Crab Race.   22

Urashimataro.   24

The Monkey and the Crab

Once upon a time, Mr. Monkey and Mrs. Crab were out for a walk. They came upon a rice ball that had fallen on the road.

"Look at what I've found!" cried Mrs. Crab happily. "Mmmmm, it sure looks good!"

Mr. Monkey was jealous. "I've got to find something, too," he muttered. And when he searched the road carefully, he found a persimmon seed.

"Hey there, Mrs. Crab—wanna trade?" asked Mr. Monkey.

"Are you kidding? No way!" replied Mrs. Crab.

By this time, Mr. Monkey felt that he just had to have that rice ball. He held the persimmon seed and began to talk to himself.

"Hmmm....what a stupid crab. Just think, if she plants this one persimmon seed, she can grow a great big tree and then have as many sweet persimmons to eat as she wants!"

Mrs. Crab overheard the monkey—and suddenly, she wanted the seed!

"Okay, let's trade," she said.

"That's really smart of you, Mrs. Crab," said the monkey as he handed her the persimmon seed. He took the rice ball and in an instant gobbled it down.

"Mmmmm...that was yummy!" said Mr Monkey as he patted his stomach.

5

Mrs. Crab went home and planted the seed in her garden. She watered the seed every day, singing, "Grow, little persimmon seed, grow, grow, grow. If you don't, I'll dig you up with my hoe!"

The persimmon seed didn't want to be dug out of his warm little home, and soon it sprouted a little green plant. Mrs. Crab fed the plant carefully every day, singing, "Grow, little persimmon sprout, become a big tree. If you don't, I'll snip you at the knee!"

Not wishing to be snipped by Mrs. Crab's sharp pincers, the sprout soon grew into a great tall tree. Now the crab came to the tree holding a big sharp ax. She sang, "Grow some persimmons for me, grow, grow, grow. If you don't, I'll chop you down, you know!"

And soon the tree was covered with bright orange persimmons.

"Wow! Look at those persimmons!"
cried Mrs. Crab.

She was so happy that she tried to
climb the tree. But every time she
tried, she just came sliding back
down.

Just then, along came Mr. Monkey.

7

"Hey there, let me climb that tree for you!" he cried, and he scampered up the tree. Then he began to stuff himself with persimmons.

"That's not fair, Mr. Monkey!" cried Mrs. Crab. "Give me some persimmons too!"

"You want a persimmon? Okay, take this one!" yelled the monkey as he threw a hard green persimmon straight at Mrs. Crab.

Mrs. Crab didn't have time to duck, and the green persimmon hit her back like a stone. Her back cracked open, and she died. From inside her shell, out poured dozens of tiny baby crabs.

"Humph...will you look at that!" said the monkey, full of ripe persimmons, as he headed back home.

"Mama's been murdered!" cried the baby crabs, waving their little pincers in the air. They milled about, wailing and crying.

Then one of the baby crabs jumped up and said, "Stop it! We have to avenge our mother's death!"

"Okay," shouted all the baby crabs. "Mr. Monkey—you'd better watch out!"

The baby crabs stopped crying and saluted, raising their pincers in the air.

Just then, along came Mr. Chestnut, Mr. Wasp, and Mr. Stone Mortar.

"Hey, little crabs...what's all the fuss about?" they asked.

"Mama's been murdered by Mr. Monkey. We're going to get even with him," replied the baby crabs.

"In that case, we'll go along with you—we'll help you!"

Everyone got in line, marching to Mr. Monkey's house. Mr. Stone Mortar thumped along, Mr. Chestnut rolled along, and Mr. Wasp buzzed along, and the baby crabs all scuttled along.

"Hey—he's not here," cried Mr. Stone Mortar. "Let's use this time to hide!"

The baby crabs hid in the water jar. The chestnut hid in the fireplace. The wasp hid in a miso jar in the kitchen. Mr. Stone Mortar hid above the door.

"Everybody be quiet now!"

In a little while, Mr. Monkey returned home, happily singing, "It's cold, it's cold—the winds from the mountain have begun to blow..."

Mr. Monkey entered his house and immediately went to the fireplace. He turned his back to the coals, trying to warm himself. And Mr. Chestnut, who had been hiding there, popped out and burned the monkey's backside!

"Ow, ow, ow!" cried the monkey. He ran to the kitchen and opened the miso jar to put some of the paste on his burn. But out flew Mr. Wasp who stung him on the nose!

"Ow, ow, ow!" shrieked the monkey. He ran to the water jar to cool his nose off. When he lifted the lid, the baby crabs leaped out, pinching him everywhere. "This is for our mother, you terrible monkey!"

"Help, help me please!" cried Mr. Monkey.

The monkey shook the baby crabs off and started to run outside, holding onto his nose and his backside. But just as he got to the door, Mr. Stone Mortar jumped down and landed right on top of him.

And that was the end of Mr. Monkey.

The Gold Coin Drying Field

Long ago there lived a young man who didn't have a job—all he did was eat and sleep. His family called him Sleepyhead.

On a beautiful sunny autumn day, his mother scolded him, "Why don't you go to help with the harvest?" Sleepyhead headed for the mountain, deciding that he might as well do as his mother said. The sun shone brightly, and the sky was deep blue.

"What a beautiful day!" said Sleepyhead when he got to the field in the mountain. He lay down in the field to take a quick nap—and just then, he heard a funny song coming from the grassy area in front of him.

> "Drying the gold coins—treasure of the mice,
>   Hurry, hurry before the cat's in the field of rice!"

Lots of mice suddenly appeared, carrying many gold coins out into the field and arranging them in neat rows.

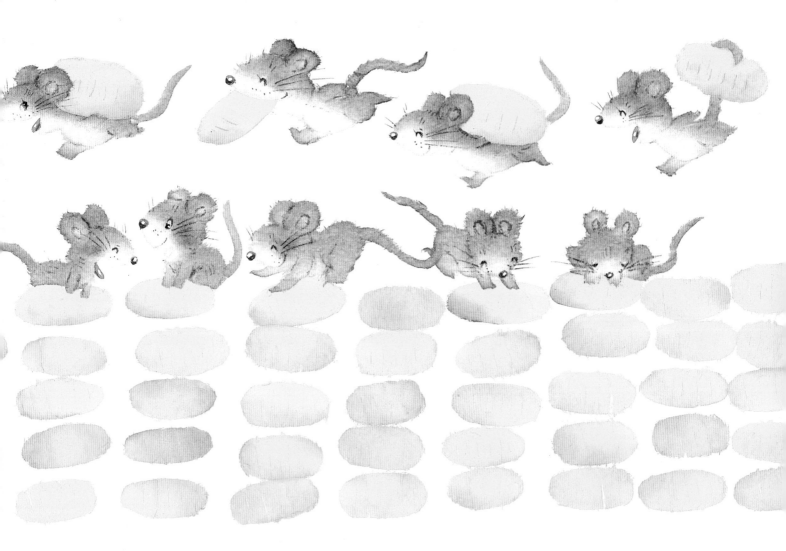

Soon the whole area became a shining gold carpet. "Wow, it's like I'm sleeping on top of a golden treasure!" thought Sleepyhead. He just stared at the coins all day until the sun began to set, and a cold wind began to blow.

Just then, the mice again appeared.

"Drying the gold coins—treasure of the mice,
  Hurry, hurry before the cat's in the field of rice!"

They sang as they began to gather the coins. When Sleepyhead struggled to his feet, the coins were all gone—not one remained!

"Well then—I guess I might as well head home," said Sleepyhead.

That evening, a beautiful young woman came to Sleepyhead's house. She carried a large basket.

"This is to thank Sleepyhead for guarding our treasure," she said. The basket was filled with gold coins, and the beautiful young woman disappeared into the night.

Gonbei the Duck Hunter

Long ago there lived a man named Gonbei who spent his days hunting ducks. One day Gonbei thought to himself, "Just catching one or two ducks a day is such a waste—I should try to catch 100 at a time.

So Gonbei went to the marsh and set 100 traps. The following morning he found 99 ducks caught in the traps!

"Hey, hey—all I need to do is wait for one more duck. Then I'll have 100!" Gonbei sat down, holding onto the 100 strings that were attached to the traps. And he waited. And he waited. And he waited. Soon the sun rose, and the water in the marsh sparkled in the sunlight. Just then, all 99 ducks flew up into the sky!

"Whoa! What's going on!" cried Gonbei. He pulled hard on the strings to try to stop the ducks, but they kept flying up and up. Soon Gonbei was in the sky as well.

Gonbei flew over fields and over mountains—higher and higher. All of a sudden, the strings that Gonbei was holding onto snapped. And like a falling kite, he fell down, down, down into a rice field.

"Wow, look at that! That man came flying down from heaven!" exclaimed the farmer working in the field. Gonbei explained what had happened, and the farmer said, "Well, you won't be able to return to your home right away. You might as well work here for a while." And so Gonbei stayed with the farmer.

One day, Gonbei was out in a field, harvesting rice. He came to one magical stalk of rice. When he tried to cut it, the stalk suddenly flew into the air, carrying Gonbei up past the mountains. This time, Gonbei fell to earth right in front of an umbrella maker's shop. So he decided to work for the umbrella maker.

A few days later, he was drying a newly-made umbrella when a strong wind began to blow. And once again, Gonbei was swept up into the sky, holding the umbrella. As he flew through the sky, he spotted the roof of a nearby temple. Just then, the wind died down and Gonbei found himself standing on the roof.

"Whew! That was lucky!" said a relieved Gonbei.

But when he looked down, he realized he was at the very top of a five story pagoda!

"He-he-help me, somebody, please!" he cried, clinging to the pagoda for dear life. Soon a crowd of people gathered at the foot of the pagoda.

Some monks from the temple brought out a big square blanket. They yelled "Jump here!" to Gonbei. But he was too afraid to jump. And while he was shaking and trembling, his feet slipped—boom! He landed headfirst right in the middle of the blanket.

The monks who were holding onto each corner of the blanket were all pulled to the middle by Gonbei's landing—bam! Their heads collided with a bang, and they all saw stars!

21

The Cat and Crab Race

One day, a cat and a crab met by the riverside.

"Hey there, Mr. Crab. You're really good at scuttling sideways, but I bet you can't run as fast as I can," said the cat proudly.

The crab replied, "We'll never know who's faster unless we race each other, will we?"

"Okay—let's race over to that rock!" said the cat, and he prepared to run.

At that moment, the crab latched onto the cat's tail with his pincers. The cat took off, running as fast as he could—and he didn't know that the crab was right on his tail!

The cat arrived at the rock in a minute. The crab let go of the cat's tail and quickly climbed up on the rock.

"Hey, Mr. Cat, you're pretty slow!" said the crab.

Surprised, the cat looked behind him.

Wh-wh-where did you come from?" he asked, terribly disappointed. "I apologize—I was no match for you!"

Urashimataro

Long ago a young man named Urashimataro lived in a village by the sea with his mother. One day as he headed for the ocean to do his usual fishing, he came across some children who had caught a little turtle. They were hitting and kicking the helpless turtle.

"How terrible!" said Urashimataro, feeling sorry for the turtle. He chased the children away and scolded them, saying, "Don't ever treat a turtle that way again!"

Urashimataro released the turtle into the ocean. The turtle swam happily off, often looking back at Urashimataro as if to thank him.

Several days later, Urashimataro was fishing from the top of a big rock.

"Excuse me, Urashimataro," he heard a voice call. Surprised, he looked down and saw a great big turtle in the water below.

"Thank you so much for helping the little turtle. As a reward, I will take you to the castle under the sea. How'd you like to ride on my back?"

And sure enough, the turtle swam underwater and took Urashimataro to a beautiful castle. The castle had a golden roof and silver walls. When they entered the gate, a beautiful princess appeared.

"Thank you for coming," she said in a lovely, lilting voice.

She was so beautiful that Urashimataro was speechless. The princess led him into the castle where the walls were made of gold and silver and the floor of jade. Atop a large platform decorated with pearls, there was mountainous feast.

"Please enjoy yourself," the princess said, as she poured him some wine. It was the first time in his life that he had ever eaten such delicious food!

Soon music began and girls dressed in gorgeous robes came out to dance. Urashimataro forgot all about his family and home—all he could do was watch the show before him.

27

The dreamlike days continued one after another. One day, however, Urashimataro suddenly remembered his mother.

"Thank you so much for everything, but I really must head home," he said to the princess.

She looked very sad and replied, "I had hoped that you would stay here forever...But I guess it can't be helped."

Then the princess gave him a beautiful lacquer box.

"Please think of me whenever you look at this box. Take very good care of it. No matter what happens, don't open it!" she warned.

"Thank you. I will never ever forget you," pledged Urashimataro. And he left the underwater castle.

The next thing he knew, he was standing on the familiar beach near his home. He rushed to his village—but when he got there, he couldn't find his house or his mother!

"What's wrong," he said, very puzzled. He walked here and there in the village that had changed so much. He didn't meet a single person he recognized, and each person he asked about his mother or his neighbors just shook his head.

Urashimataro returned to the beach, carrying his precious lacquer box. "If I'd known it was going to be this bad, I would never have come back," he said sadly.

He forgot all about his promise to the princess and opened the box. A huge white cloud rose from inside the box—in an instant, Urashimataro became a very old man! The short time he thought he had spent under the ocean was really 100 years!

A NOTE TO PARENTS:
Capturing a Child's Imagination

Children are just full of curiosity. They're always looking about expectantly, wanting to discover new things. The more they learn, the wider their eyes open to find what interests them.

A child's interest in books begin with wordless picture books, then turns to picture books with stories. Though some children may read and interpret these storybooks on their own, most must rely on an adult to help read and interpret the stories for them. During this important period of development, it is critical for children to have stories read aloud to them by an adult. A child's mother and father are the adults who are the closest and most dear to the child. Indeed, hearing the loving voice of a mother or father telling (and retelling) a story can become one of the child's most reassuring memories. In addition, by reading stories aloud, parents enrich their child's imagination. Just as food provides nutrition for the child's growing body, the interchange between child and parent during storytelling can be a nutrient for the mind and soul.

The collection of stories in this volume include some of Japan's most cherished tales. As with all fables and legends, it isn't clear where, by whom, or even when these stories were composed. Most likely, the tales grew out of the daily lives of our ancestors and from generation to generation, were passed from parent to child. What is clear about the fairy tales, however, is their value. Whose imagination wouldn't be captivated by a witty animal race, the adventures of a duck hunter, a magical kingdom beneath the sea and other stories of the fantastic? But the *Japanese Fairy Tales* are more than just entertaining; they also address some of life's enduring themes: How to live a good, kind life; how to achieve happiness; and the price to be paid for cruelty, greediness, and cowardice. Through these tales, then, and through the humorous way in which they are told, children learn human virtue and traditional wisdom.

Keisuke Nishimoto, Professor
Showa Woman's College
Tokyo, Japan